D1286875

WINNIPEG
JUL 22 2005
PUBLIC LIBRARY

THE LAST WOLF

www.booksattransworld.co.uk/childrens

Also available by Michael Morpurgo

Tom's Sausage Lion

Black Queen
illustrated by Tony Ross

The Rainbow Bear
illustrated by Michael Foreman

The Silver Swan
illustrated by Christian Birmingham

The Last Wolf

MICHAEL MORPURGO

illustrated by Michael Foreman

DOUBLEDAY
London New York Toronto Sydney Auckland

TRANSWORLD PUBLISHERS
61–63 Uxbridge Road, London W5 5SA
A division of The Random House Group Ltd

RANDOM HOUSE AUSTRALIA (PTY) LTD
20 Alfred Street, Milsons Point, Sydney
New South Wales 2061, Australia

RANDOM HOUSE NEW ZEALAND LTD
18 Poland Road, Glenfield, Auckland 10, New Zealand

RANDOM HOUSE (PTY) LTD
Endulini, 5a Jubilee Road, Parktown 2193, South Africa

Published in 2002 by Doubleday
a division of Transworld Publishers

1 3 5 7 9 10 8 6 4 2

This story was specially commissioned by Tate Britain and was performed during the Ilkley Festival 2001.

A catalogue record for this book is available from the British Library.

ISBN 0 385 602227

Typeset in Palatino by
Phoenix Typesetting, Ilkley, West Yorkshire

Printed in Great Britain by
Mackays of Chatham, Chatham, Kent

For Neil and Gill – MM

Miya's New-fangled Machine

'You're an ostrich, Grandpa,' Miya told me, sitting herself down on my bed and peeling an orange for me.

'And why's that then?' I asked her.

'Because whenever you see something you don't like, you just bury your head in the sand and pretend it's not there.'

It was an old argument between us, not that you'd call it an argument as such, more of a tease.

But whatever it was, I knew that sooner rather than later she was going to wear me down. Miya was determined to drag me into the twenty-first century whether I liked it or not. And now she'd found the perfect opportunity.

'You've got nothing else to do, Grandpa,' she went on. 'You're bored out of your mind. Why not try it, at least? I'll come in and teach you, if you like, every evening. Won't take long. It's easy-peasy – nothing to be frightened of.'

'I'm not frightened,' I replied. 'I just don't see the point of all these new-fangled machines, that's all.'

'Like I said, you're an ostrich. Here.' She gave me my orange. 'Eat. It's good for you,' she said. 'Listen, Grandpa, it's brilliant, honest it is. There's millions of different things you can do on it – e-mail, word processing, games, shopping . . .'

'I hate shopping,' I told her.

'You're a grumpy old ostrich too,' she said, bending over to kiss me on the cheek. 'We'll get started tomorrow. I'll bring over my laptop, all right? Byeee!'

And she was out of the door and gone, ignoring all my protests. She had won.

All this came about because I'd been ill – just flu at first, but then it became pneumonia. The doctor, who's a good friend of mine as well as my doctor, wagged his finger at me, and said, 'Now you listen to me, Michael McLeod, this is serious. You're no spring chicken any more. You've got to stay in bed, and in the warm. No more gardening, no more golf, no more fishing. You've got to look after yourself.' So, cooped up in my flat for weeks on end, I had become, as Miya had so rightly diagnosed, bored out of my mind.

Miya was fourteen, my eldest granddaughter and the apple of my eye. She was always popping in to cheer me up, bless her – she lives just round the corner. And she did cheer me up too, even if she did go on and on about the joys of her wretched computer. The truth was that so long as she came to see me, I didn't mind what we did, or what she talked about. It would pass the time, and talking about computers made a welcome change from losing to her at chess – again.

The computer lessons did not start well. I just could not get my head around it all. Then, bit by bit, day by day, with Miya's help, I began to make some sense of it; and once I'd made sense of it, I began to enjoy it – much to my surprise. A couple of weeks later Miya went off on her summer holidays, leaving me strict instructions as to how to plug in and keep in touch with her by e-mail. She told me I must promise to practise every day on the computer. I promised, and I like to keep my promises.

So, except for occasional check-up visits from my doctor friend, and from my neighbour who very kindly did all my shopping for me, I was left alone in the house with Miya's computer. One morning, as I sat there in front of it, about to switch on, I began asking myself why I was doing this. I mean, what was this machine really for? What could it do for me? How, now I'd begun to master it, could I use it to help me through the long days of convalescence that still lay ahead of me? I needed a project, I thought. Something to occupy my mind, something I could really get my teeth into, and something this computer could help me to achieve.

I had a sudden idea. It was an old idea, one I'd

had in the back of my mind for many years, but had never bothered to do anything much about. This was my opportunity. I had the time, and now I had the means – literally at my fingertips. I would set out on a quest, a quest I could achieve without ever leaving the flat. I could do it all, the whole thing, on the Internet, by e-mail. I would search out my roots, piece together my family tree, discover where I came from, who I came from. I would trace my family line back as far as I could go.

On my mother's side, the Meredith side, this proved simple enough because they had lived in this country, in Suffolk mostly, for many generations, and I could track them down through parish records, through registers of births and marriages and deaths. I managed to trace that side of the family all the way back to a Hannah Meredith, who I discovered had been baptized in Southwold on 2 May 1730.

It was like detective work, genealogical detective work, and I was soon completely engrossed in it. I was e-mailing dozens of times a day. I had all the information I had gathered on a database. Miya and I exchanged e-mails often, particularly when I got stuck and needed her help. As Miya had said, her computer was 'brilliant', utterly 'brilliant'.

But my father's family, the McLeod side, the Scottish side, proved much more difficult to trace even with the help of the computer, because they had moved about the world, one of the family to Argentina, one to Australia and another to the United States of America. Only a few generations back the trails kept going cold, and I was beginning to feel very frustrated. I simply had no more clues to follow up, not a single one.

Then, thank goodness, Miya came back home from her holiday and to my rescue. She told me I should upload my whole family tree onto a genealogical website, and appeal for help that way. So that's what I did. For several days I had no response at all. Then one evening Miya logged on for me and found an e-mail from Marianne McLeod of Boston, Massachusetts, in the United States.

She had, she wrote, studied my father's side of my family tree with great interest and felt sure we must be distant cousins. She, like me, had been researching her family background – she called it her 'lifelong obsession' – and had traced her family to Scotland, as far back as the 1700s, to her ancestor, and mine, she hoped – one Robbie McLeod of Inverness-shire. Quite by chance she had recently discovered hidden away amongst her family papers, Robbie McLeod's last will and testament. *It's the most wonderful story I have ever read. I've scanned it into my computer. Would you like to see it?* Would I! I e-mailed back to her at once. *Greetings, distant cousin, I can't wait.* Miya was as excited as I was now. There was no reply until nearly twenty-four hours later. Miya was there beside me when I first read it. One glance told me that it had been worth waiting for. As I read, my heart in my mouth with excitement, I knew that my quest had been achieved, that with the help of Miya's new-fangled machine, Miya and I had discovered something quite wonderful, as wonderful as any holy grail. I was reading the last words, in his own handwriting, of my great-great-great-great-great-grandfather. He was speaking to us from across the ages.

THE LAST WISHES OF ROBBIE McLEOD

❧

WRIT BY MY OWN HAND THIS THIRD DAY OF DECEMBER IN THE YEAR SEVENTEEN HUNDRED AND NINETY-FIVE, BEING NEAR THE END OF MY LIFE, BUT OF SOUND MIND.

I leave all that I have in this world, all of Burnside Farm, all my sheep and horses, all my possessions, Captain McKinnon's musket, all my goods and chattels, such as they be, to my dear son Alan, who has been as good a son to me as any man could ever desire.

Furthermore, in the belief that the lives we lead must surely serve as the most valuable legacy we can leave to those who come after us, I shall endeavour to set down the extraordinary events that have shaped my life and brought me to this place.

I did not come here alone, nor did I come by chance. Without the last wolf I should never be here at all. Without the last wolf I should have been another man entirely. I owe all I am, all I have in this life to the last wolf. This therefore is his story as much as it is mine, and so I have entitled it:

❧

THE LAST WOLF

I never knew my mother nor my father. It was always told to me by my Uncle Archibald, who was my guardian – and my tormentor too – that my mother, his sister, was a wilful wicked woman, and my father a ne'er-do-well sailor who had been lost at sea when I was still a bairn. Within a year of his death, my poor mother had died also, leaving me an orphan. Thus I came to pass my wretched childhood at my Uncle Archibald's house in Inverness-shire, far from all other human habitation, a forbidding grey fortress of a place that never saw sunlight nor ever heard the sound of laughter.

Try as I did to please him, scarce a day passed when he did not reproach me. 'Out of the kindness of my heart, and because I am a good and Christian soul, I took pity on you. And thus you repay me.' This was ever his constant refrain as he beat me for my dire sins, and dreadful misdemeanours. Indeed, he used me more as a slave than a nephew, compelling me to wait on him in the house, to work for him on the farm, keeping me in such a state of abject misery and hunger and terror that at last I could endure it no longer and ran away. So it was that I found myself at scarcely twelve years of age wandering the world alone and quite destitute.

For many months, close to starvation, I roamed the hills and glens of the Highlands, hunting and scavenging for my food like some wild beast. Finding no other means to sustain myself, I was obliged to steal whatever I could find to keep body and soul together. I fared little better when I left the countryside and ventured into the dark and crowded streets of Edinburgh. Here too I was reduced to thieving and beggary, and several times barely avoided capture.

Cold and hunger drove me to ever more desperate and hazardous escapades. Caught one morning in the very act of thieving a loaf of bread from a baker's shop, I was pursued through the streets by an angry, howling mob past the Palace of Holyrood and out into the hills beyond where at last, to my great relief, they gave up the chase.

After this I dared not return for fear I might be recognized. Some days later, weak with a fever and near to death I stumbled into a stable and lay down, never, I thought, to rise again. But fortune at last smiled upon me. I had happened by chance upon two of the kindest, most generous souls that ever lived, who finding me barely alive in their stable, took me in and cared for me.

Sean Dunbar and his good wife Mary had no child of their own and from the very beginning thought of me as their true son. Being devout believers they could not doubt but that I had been sent to them as a gift from God. 'Did we not pray for just such a miracle? Did we not find you in a stable, Robbie?' Mary said, and indeed repeated it often, marvelling at it each time. 'And were you not curled up in the straw like Jesus himself in Bethlehem?'

They set good food before me and put warm clothes on my back, and so restored me in time to strength and health. They breathed happiness into me, such happiness as I had never known existed, the greatest happiness there can be on this earth – that is, to be loved and cherished. I worked alongside Sean in his smithy, holding the horses for him, stoking the fire, and was soon a skilled apprentice. I can mind he always sung as he worked, in time with the strike of the hammer. Thus it was that I learned all manner of songs I had never heard before, stirring songs of rebellion, songs I have never forgot since, even to this day.

And Mary, poor dear Mary, whom I came to love like a mother, taught me to read and write and to say my prayers at night-time. 'Speak always to the Lord, Robbie, and softly, before you close your eyes in sleep, for one day His will surely be the face you see when you wake. Pray to Him. He will always listen, and He will always understand. And besides which, He likes it. He likes it when we speak to Him. Remember that.' So I prayed each night. But though I never told her so, I much preferred to talk to her than to the Lord. She it was who gave me all the love and understanding I needed, and taught me right from wrong too. No mother could have done more for a son.

As for Sean, he was as much a friend to me as a father, the first true friend I ever had. I saw in my two beloved benefactors all that is good and fine in human nature. I had found a safe and happy haven with them, a home where I knew I belonged. But my new-found happiness was not to last. Cruel circumstance snatched it from me and set me on a course towards new and ever more terrible dangers.

I had been with them no more than three short years when Bonnie Prince Charlie's army came marching by, marching south against the English, with their drums beating bravely and their flags fluttering so fair and so proud. When they made camp nearby I myself was called upon to shoe Bonnie Prince Charlie's horse. A fine horse he was too, but his master was finer still, clad like a highland prince and tall as a god. Around the campfires that night we sang their songs and danced their dances. By morning both Sean and I, and many others from the village too, were quite resolved upon our decision. We would join him. We would be marching into England with Bonnie Prince Charlie's army.

Poor Mary did all in her power to prevent us. She wept on Sean's shoulder, and begged him not to go. 'Have we found a son at last only to lose him?' she cried. 'And what for? For the skirl of the pipes, is it? To kill a few English lads, sons like Robbie who have mothers like me, fathers like you, sons and fathers they will mourn all their days. Stay by me, Sean. Do not leave me.'

But Sean was as determined upon this venture as I was. He said that he was compelled by his conscience to go and fight for the liberty of his country, to set Bonnie Prince Charlie on his throne where he rightly belonged, but that I was man enough now to make up my own mind. And I, being young and foolish, lusting after excitement and adventure, and persuaded of the justice of our great cause, would have my way.

I could not look her in the eyes as I spoke. 'Where my father goes, I must go,' I told her. With these words I think I broke her heart.

So when the army left, Sean Dunbar and I went with them, and left Mary weeping at her door. We were soldiers now in the service of Bonnie Prince Charlie.

Pipes skirling, we marched into England, a spring in our step and a song in our hearts. But an army needs more than hope, more than drums and pipes and flags. A motley band, filled with fierce pride and burning zeal, but poorly fed, poorly armed and equipped, we were no match for the serried ranks of Redcoats. I only saw one battle. One, I swear, is enough for any man.

At Culloden Moor we fought the Redcoats steel against steel, the claymore against the bayonet, fought and died, fought and ran, scattered like leaves in the teeth of a cruel gale. Sean fell to his knees at my side, his breast pierced by a musket ball. He clutched at my collar, clinging to me as if I were life itself.

'Mary was right,' he breathed, 'We shouldn't have come. I shouldn't have brought you to this dreadful place. Run, Robbie, run while you can. There's no more you can do for me. Save yourself.'

And on saying this he fell back dead in my arms.

To my everlasting shame I left him lying there and ran from the field. But unlike so many of my poor comrades, who were hunted down and slaughtered by the Redcoats, I made good my escape. I was mercifully unwounded, fleet of foot and artful. I made for home, hiding up by day, and moving only at night under cover of darkness, but I arrived home only to discover that the accursed Redcoats had been there before me.

Those that were left told me the terrible story, how the Redcoats had come and razed the village to the ground, how they had cut down everyone who resisted.

'What of Mary?' I cried. 'What of my mother?'

They would not reply, but brought me instead to the churchyard and showed me her grave newly dug and her name carved upon a wooden cross.

I could scarcely believe what my eyes were seeing.

'You'd best be gone, Robbie,' they told me, 'for the Redcoats will be back. They're hanging all the rebels they find. Be gone, Robbie, be gone while you can.'

Orphaned once more, bereaved and bereft, I fled north to the Highlands. Here, maddened with grief, I lived wild again, not daring to venture into any human company for fear of betrayal and discovery, for fear of the dreaded Redcoats who, like an army of invading ants, had occupied and infested every corner of our land. Once caught they would spare me no mercy – of that I was quite certain.

I lay low in the mountains for many long and dreary weeks, and would have stayed there longer, for I knew the danger had not yet passed. But there in those bare and inhospitable mountains I could find little to eat but berries and roots, scarce enough to keep body and soul alive. Hunger it was that drove me at last down into the glens. At night, I went from farm to farm, from village to village, stealing what little food I could find. By the coming of every dawn I would find some barn or byre where I thought I might safely sleep away the daylight hours. But it was in just such a barn that I was at last discovered. The farm dog must have found me out, for he set up such a hullabaloo of howling and barking that the farmer came running from the house with his blunderbuss.

Again I ran for the hills and thought at first I had escaped clean away. But looking back over my shoulder I saw to my horror a troop of Redcoats riding out after me in hot pursuit. I knew now that I must surely be caught and killed, for the open hillside afforded little place to hide myself. But when death threatens, a man will do all he must to survive. I found strength where there had been none, and ran on and on until at last my legs would carry me no further, and I fell on my knees in the heather. A fusillade of shots echoed through the glen. I closed my eyes and waited for death, praying only that it would be quick.

But when at last the echoes died away and I found myself still alive, I opened my eyes, and looked back. The troop of Redcoats was galloping along the ridge of the hill on the far side of the glen, and following them any number of villagers on horse and on foot, all whooping with the excitement of the hunt. To my utter joy and amazement I could see now that they had not been hunting me at all, but were after quite another quarry, one I could not rightly discern for it was far away, and sprang so swiftly through the heather, at once too big for a fox, and too small for a deer.

Both quarry and hunters were soon gone away over the crest of the hill, leaving me on my knees and thanking God in His mercy for my lucky escape. But my prayers of thanksgiving were interrupted by the sound of more shooting, a thunderous volley that clattered about the glen, and was followed by the emptiness of a terrible and ominous silence. I heard then, resounding through

the hills, the same triumphant blood-curdling yell I had heard on the battlefield at Culloden Moor when the Redcoats had charged us and put us to flight. I knew that the hunt had made its kill, and I pitied the unfortunate beast whatever it was, and thanked God most fervently that it was not me.

I lay still on the heather for some time and watched the Redcoats and the hunters returning to the village, the poor creature swinging from a pole. At dusk a mist came down over the hills and hid me from their sight, after which I felt it safe enough to

move. I made my way down the glen, across the tumbling burn and up over the steep hillside beyond where the hunt had made their kill. This was my only way out, for there was, I knew, a high and impassable mountain at my back and a village full of Redcoats below me, both of which I knew I must avoid. So I set out southwards along a rough trail, having now no idea where I should go, only that I must put as much distance between myself and the troop of Redcoats as I could.

I had not gone far when I came upon a great flat rock, and freshly painted in blood upon it, I found these words, which I read in the last glimmer of day: *Near this rock was killed the last wolf in Scotland. 24 April 1746.*

I knew not if this claim were true or false. Indeed, at that time I knew little enough of wolves, only that by repute the wolf was a species of wild and savage dog that stalked the countryside, preying on sheep, and even sometimes, it was believed, on human flesh, so that whenever and wherever they were found they were mercilessly hunted down and killed.

As I stood there contemplating how strange it was that my own life had been saved by such a creature, I heard at some small distance from me in the dark of the heather the sound of whining and yelping. Within a dozen paces I came upon what I perceived at once to be a wolf pup. I was not fearful for I could see that he was too weak to do me harm. Neither, it seemed, was he in the least fearful of me. He paid me not the slightest heed when I crouched over him, but instead licked the ground, crying piteously as though his heart would break. I talked to him as I crouched down and gentled him.

'Come,' I said, feeling at once an instant kinship between us, the kinship of orphans, the kinship of fugitives, 'this is no place for you. This is no place for either of us. I live now only because your mother died. So I shall care for you as she would. That much I owe her. That much I owe you. You are alone in this world as I am. But if we are together then we are not alone, are we? We shall go where we go always together. Trust me.'

With some difficulty, for he was heavier than I had thought, I gathered him up and held him in my arms. Though he struggled against me, and snarled and snapped, he was not strong enough to do me much hurt. 'And I shall call you Charlie,' I told him, 'for you are bonnie, and a prince among wolves.'

From that day on, I had always two mouths to feed, two reasons to survive, and therefore my resolve to do so was redoubled. I passed the long summer months hidden away with Charlie in a deserted croft high in the hills, living only on what I could catch or trap from the streams and hills about me. Being summer, there were rabbits and hares enough, and trout too in the burn. And Charlie needed little encouragement to eat. The more I fed him, the more he came to trust me. Though I looked for it at first, and feared it too, I saw in him no sign of a wolf's reputed savagery. He curled his lip and bared his teeth at me only in jest as we played together. And play indeed we did, romping and rolling in the heather, wrestling with one another like children. Even when he bit me, he bit only gently, in affection, leaving me with raw knuckles perhaps, but with no real hurt ever done to me.

He grew quickly from a pup into a young wolf, and as he did so came to know me and to love me, perceiving me now as his provider and his friend, so that he would follow me wherever I went, his nose touching the back of my leg as if to remind me constantly of his presence, of his reliance upon me,

of his affection for me. In my turn, I came to look upon Charlie as my only friend in a world full of enemies. I had no other. Wolf and rebel, we were inseparably bound together by the very nature of our common plight. So it was Charlie I talked to, Charlie I confided in, and like the good friend he was, he seemed always ready and willing to listen.

The summer months passed into autumn and we were still undisturbed in our remote hideaway in the hills. But with time to brood and winter approaching I was becoming ever more anxious about our predicament. To survive a winter in this barren place would be hard, and I feared too that even here we must surely one day be discovered and hunted down, that our good fortune, which had held for so long could not last much longer. I began to realize that if we were not to remain fugitives in these hills all our days, I must find some more permanent home elsewhere, across the sea , in some more hospitable land, in France perhaps. Some Frenchmen had fought bravely alongside us at Culloden, so I knew that the French were sympathetic to our rebellion and might give us sanctuary.

I had only once seen the sea, in Edinburgh. I remembered the ships lying at anchor, so I determined to return there as soon as possible. I thought we might be able to lose ourselves in amongst the great crowds that thronged the streets. But even here I knew I could scarce expect to remain unnoticed for long with Charlie at my side.

Tame though he was now, and biddable too, and in many respects much like any other large dog, there could be no doubt that Charlie did indeed by this time resemble what in fact he unmistakably was, a wolf. I knew well enough that almost no creature is more instantly recognizable than a wolf, and that none inspires more fear, nor more hatred either. Discovery would mean certain death for both of us, wolf and rebel alike, a circumstance I tried to explain to Charlie as I set about the business of disguising him.

I think I should never have discovered how this might be accomplished at all, had my eye not fallen one evening on a pair of discarded sheep shears hanging on the wall of the croft. I burned the rust off in the fire, sharpened the sheep shears on a stone, and set to work at once on Charlie. But

Charlie made it plain that this was an indignity he deeply resented. He would growl at me and back away, refusing to stand still for me. Knowing that I could not restrain him against his will, for he was by now far too strong for me, I resorted to bribery, as I so often did with Charlie. I discovered that if I coaxed him almost constantly with rabbit meat he would, albeit unwillingly, stand and endure the sheep shears.

Until I began to cut his hair, I never imagined a wolf could grow so much of it and so thick. When, after some hours, I had done with my clipping, Charlie had taken on the appearance more of a bedraggled deerhound than a wolf. Although on close examination, his great webbed feet and his amber eyes might betray him, I was satisfied that he no longer had the shape and form of a wolf, that he might indeed pass for a large hound. I can mind how he stood there shivering in his humiliation and looking up at me out of baleful, accusing eyes, his tail between his legs. I would not, I thought, be easily forgiven. In this I was mistaken. It seemed not to be in Charlie's nature to bear a grudge, and very soon we were once again the best of friends.

So, as the first flurries of snow fell about the croft, we left and travelled south to Edinburgh. Happily our journey proved less perilous that I had feared. We saw fewer Redcoats that I had expected, and passed by unchallenged wherever we went, save only once. We encountered a traveller, sitting drunk by the wayside, and he stopped us, saying he had never in all his life set eyes upon such a strange looking creature as Charlie.

'There is something wolfish about him,' said he. 'If he had more hair on him, I'd swear he was a wolf.' I spoke not a word in reply, but waved cheerily, and passed on by without looking back, hoping against hope that he would not come after us. Thankfully he did not, and so I breathed again.

Once in the bustling streets of the city, I discovered that my earlier supposition had been justified, that there was indeed some safety in numbers, for no-one paid us any heed at all. By good chance I soon found work in a sailmaker's loft on the dockside at Leith, and basement lodgings nearby. The place was rat-infested, but did not remain so for long, for Charlie soon hunted them to extinction. The sailmaking was arduous and long, and the pay scarcely sufficient. Yet we had a roof over our heads and the wherewithal to feed ourselves. We had much to be thankful for.

Still wary of discovery, I did not frequent the seamen's taverns, and so far as was practicable, withdrew from all human company for fear that one of us might reveal himself for what he was. At the approach of any Redcoat – and there were always Redcoats aplenty down by the port in Leith – I would pass by on the other side averting my eyes from their gaze.

Each evening in the quiet of our lodgings I would trim Charlie's hair so that I might maintain his disguise. He had by now become quite accustomed to this ritual, standing quite still for the shears as if he understood the need for it. I would tell him, as I clipped him, of my hopes and my dreams, of how we would one day find a ship and sail away to some far distant shore where neither of us would be hunted, where we might be free to roam without threat or hindrance wherever we wished. I worked for it by day in the heat of the sail loft, dreamed of it constantly and prayed for it on my knees at night, as poor dead Mary had taught me. Had she not told me that God would always be listening? I do not think I ever quite believed her, until the day I met Captain McKinnon.

Late each evening with the streets empty of people, it was my custom to take Charlie for a walk. On one such evening in summer I had paused, as I often did, and was gazing out to sea, with Charlie at my side, when I encountered a stranger, or rather I should say that he encountered me. By his dress I could see he was a gentleman and a sea captain. By the direct look in his eyes, I perceived at once that he was an honest man. But nonetheless I was on my guard as I always was with strangers. I did not yet know it, but this was the man who was to change the course of my life, and Charlie's, for ever. He stopped nearby to light his pipe, and having done so engaged me in friendly conversation.

'It's a fine-looking hound you have there, my lad,' he said, 'if indeed that is what it is.'

'What do you mean by that, sir?' I asked, at once alarmed.

'I mean that unless my eyes deceive me, that is as close to being a wolf as any dog I've ever clapped eyes on,' said the sea captain.

'But there are no wolves in Scotland,' I insisted, 'not any more.'

'Maybe not,' he replied. 'But we have Redcoats aplenty in their place, do we not? If you understand my meaning.' The look we exchanged was one of silent conspiracy, of immediate and mutual understanding. I knew then I need harbour no more suspicions of this man, that I had nothing whatsoever to fear from him.

'I have seen you sitting here often of an evening, you and your hound, side by side,' the sea captain went on. 'And always you look far out to sea as if you long to go there. Am I right in this?' I could not deny it. The sea captain's eyes glowed in the light of his pipe. 'Where is it you wish to go? To France? To America perhaps? I have seen wolves in America, bigger than this hound of yours maybe, and with a thicker coat, but much the same. I tell you, he has the same eyes as they do. He has the eyes of a wolf.'

'You know America, sir?' I asked, seeking to divert his gaze and his attention from Charlie. 'You have been there?'

'Aye, I have been there many a time,' said he. 'It is a country as close to paradise as you'll find on this earth. You should go there. Every man should go there. You should see it for yourself. Thousands of miles of wilderness. I tell you, a man could lose himself in such a place. There is peace to be found there, peace and prosperity too; aye and, besides these, the one thing a man needs and desires most of all.'

'And what might that be?' I asked him.

'Freedom,' said the sea captain, and as he spoke he looked me in the eye so hard, so deep that I thought he might read my very soul. 'If it is freedom you seek, my lad, as I believe it might be, then perhaps I may be of some service to you.' He lifted his cap. 'Pray allow me to introduce myself. My name is Captain McKinnon. I am master of the *Pelican*, the two-masted brig you see over yonder at the quay-side. We sail within a few days, first to France, to Bordeaux, with a cargo of wool, and thence to America

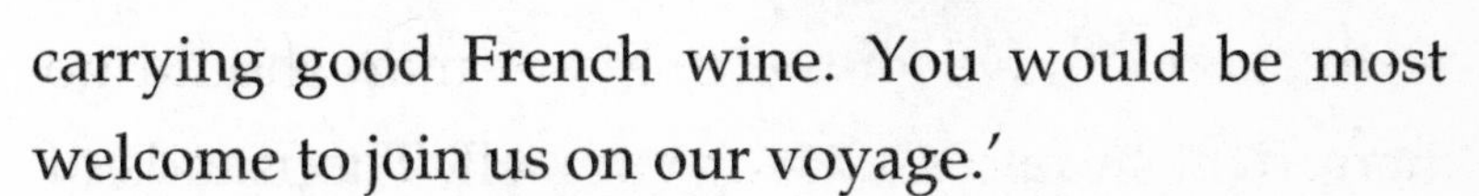

carrying good French wine. You would be most welcome to join us on our voyage.'

'But I have no money to pay for such a passage,' I told him.

'Did I ask you for money?' replied the sea captain. 'If you are willing to work, then I am willing to hire you. I still have need for one more good strong deckhand to crew my ship. I pay nothing, but be assured, I will feed you well, and will do all in my power to bring you safe to America.'

'If I go,' said I, 'then my dog goes with me. We stay together. I have promised him as much.'

The sea captain laughed at this and clapped me on the shoulder. 'I like your spirit, my lad,' said he. 'Well then, he can be ship's dog, can he not? He can chase off the rats. He can bark and bay at the wind and the waves. Be sure we shall have plenty of both. I've no doubt he can earn his keep. What do you say then? Will you join us?' At this he offered his hand to me, and I took it willingly, accepting his kind offer and thanking him from the very bottom of my heart.

So I joined the crew of the *Pelican* and within the week left the shores of my native country behind me for ever, with, I confess, very little sadness in my heart, for saving my few brief years with Sean and Mary I had known little but misery in the land of my birth.

I was very soon to discover just how good and noble a man was this Captain McKinnon. We had not been many hours at sea and were scarcely out of sight of the land, when he ordered the ship's hold to be opened

up. To my utter astonishment, up onto the deck came more than two dozen men, women and children, shielding their eyes against the unaccustomed brightness. All looked thin and ragged and destitute. Some stood at the ship's side and wept to see the last hills of Scotland disappear from view, but many more fell to their knees thanking God for deliverance out of the hands of their enemies.

It was evident to me that they, like me, like Charlie, like every man in the crew were followers of Bonnie Prince Charlie, Jacobite sympathizers, and every one of us fleeing for our lives. For all of us on that ship

Captain McKinnon had been our saviour and our guardian angel. This nobility of purpose was born, as I later heard, out of his own grief. His only son, being like me barely sixteen at the time, had been slain at the battle on Culloden Moor, and his poor wife had died soon after of a broken heart.

Thereafter the Captain had taken it upon himself to save all those hunted fugitives he could find and to spirit them secretly away to America and safety. I swear no braver man nor kindlier one was ever born. He proved to be a fine seaman too, able to read the waves and the weather as well and as wisely as he read men's hearts and minds, able too to avoid the ships of the English fleet that were now a constant threat to our liberty, to our very lives. With such a man as our Captain at the helm little could go amiss, I thought. But in this I was to be sorely mistaken.

Charlie was never entirely happy below decks where there was always a great press of people about us. Accustomed as we were to the wide open spaces of the Highlands, the crowded and stifling conditions of our close confinement made us both restless. So, whether I was on watch or not, we lived as much as possible, when the weather allowed, up on deck where we could breathe in the wind, where we could see the great expanse of the sky and the ocean, where we could be more alone and at our ease. There were many nights too, when, to avoid the heat and the stench below decks we would curl up together on deck and sleep under the stars, a habit my fellow fugitives found altogether incomprehensible and strange.

But as time passed I began to notice that Charlie had taken to pacing anxiously up and down the deck on his own, forever stopping and looking out to sea, longing, as I supposed, for some sight of land. I noticed too that at the approach of a storm he could always be found standing forward at the bow. There he would stay, like a sentry on duty, alert to danger, his ears pricked, his entire body trembling with anticipation and excitement. Then, on a sudden whim, and for no reason I could understand at first, he would lift his head and howl into the wind, a most baleful sound that much unnerved and upset everyone on board.

Upon hearing this, murmurings soon went about the ship that Charlie howled like a wolf, and that perhaps he might indeed be a wolf, which presumption of course I hotly denied. But my denials went unheeded. 'Devil dog' some began to call him, or 'Jonah dog'. Despite all my protestations on Charlie's behalf, all my reassurances, mothers began to keep their children away from him, and from me too, children who until now had always played quite contentedly with both of us. I found myself at first shunned, then cast out like a leper, and friendless, except it must be said for the good Captain who always remained steadfast in his kindness towards me and towards Charlie.

It was often remarked in my hearing – and I confess that I too had noticed it and was puzzled by it – that Charlie seemed to possess an unnatural power, the power to sense the approach of a storm before we did, before even the Captain himself. But some on board, those most vociferous in their suspicions of Charlie, went further than this. They put it about that in heralding a storm with his dreadful howling it must be Charlie himself who brought the storm down upon us, that he was a curse to the ship and so a threat to all who sailed in her. This rumour ran around the ship like wildfire, and served only to increase their enmity towards us, increasing my sense of rejection and isolation. Worse though was yet to come.

We had safely run the English blockade, delivered our cargo of wool to Bordeaux, and had been but a day at sea bound for America, when Charlie set up such an ominous howling from the bow of the ship that we knew a storm must be in the air, and that we must very soon be in the midst of it. The Captain had us take in the mainsail at once. We battened down and prepared ourselves as best we could for what was to come. We would have to run before the storm and endure it, the Captain said. There was nothing else to be done.

For five days without ceasing we were tossed about the ocean by seas more mountainous than I had ever thought possible. Great green waves bore down upon us, forty, fifty foot in height, waves

so powerful that I was sure they must overwhelm us and swallow us entirely. I prayed as I had never prayed before, but still the storm raged on mercilessly and roared about us in its fury. Despite all my most fervent prayers, God, it seemed, had abandoned us utterly.

One man was lost overboard, and yet another, Rory Niven it was, from Dundee, was knocked senseless below decks by the violence of the storm. He died later in his poor wife's arms. Time and again the ship came close to foundering, and more than once I resigned myself to my inevitable and imminent death. Yet throughout this prolonged nightmare Captain McKinnon remained a fine example to us all of courage and composure. He sought always to keep our spirits high, and kept us ever to our tasks, assuring us that the *Pelican* was a sound ship, that not this storm nor any other could sink her, that God in his mercy would surely protect us.

So in the end it proved. But when at long last the storm had passed us by and the skies had cleared, the blame for the storm itself and for all that had happened fell at once upon Charlie and upon me.

We were all on deck together, having just buried poor Rory at sea, when, outraged at the suffering and tragedy they had had to endure, passengers and crew alike came to the Captain in a state of high and mutinous indignation. They demanded that the Captain either turn forthwith back to France where Charlie and I must be set ashore, or else they would have no choice but to put us both out in a longboat and cast us adrift on the open ocean, the very thought of which terrified me greatly. The Captain listened in silence to all they had to say.

Then in a grave voice, his eyes ablaze with anger, he spoke his mind.

'Shame on you, I say,' he began. 'Shame on all of you. I had until now thought better of you, but I see I was much mistaken. Have we escaped the cruelty of the Redcoats only to inflict the very same cruelty on one another? Wolf or no wolf, Charlie is as much God's creature as any of us and has done none of us harm. I have vowed to bring both him and you safe to America and this, God willing, I shall accomplish. I have sailed these seas all my life and have sailed through many such savage storms.

It is not Charlie who brings these storms upon us. Such talk is born of nothing but ignorant superstition and wanton foolishness. It is the winds and the

tides, I tell you. It is the elements themselves that conspire with one another to stir the waves into such a fury. No indeed. I shall not do as you bid me. It is I who am Captain of this ship and I shall not return to France, no matter how you threaten me. And if you dare to abandon them in the longboat, then you must cast me adrift also, for I would rather perish with them than live in the company of such unworthy people.'

Not one of them dared raise a voice against him. Stung by the fury of his passion, they stole away shamefaced. After that, whether storm-tossed or becalmed, I never again heard whisperings against Charlie, no, nor none against me either. With the passing of time my companions seemed to forget

the matter entirely and warmed to us once more. The children played with Charlie as they had before, and took to howling with him too, so that it sounded sometimes as if we had not one wolf on board the *Pelican* but an entire pack.

We talked amongst each other constantly now of our great hopes for our new life in America. Many of my fellow fugitives had been driven by the Redcoats from their sheep farms in Scotland and would be seeking new lands in America where they might once again graze their sheep and live out their lives in peace and tranquillity. After much consideration, and on the good Captain's advice, I decided that I too might follow this course. There was, Captain McKinnon assured me, land enough and plenty for everyone, 'a great and wonderful unexplored wilderness' he called it. So I determined I would settle somewhere deep in this great wilderness of America and make a farm of my own. Thus, I thought, Charlie and I could continue to live together unnoticed and far from the inquisitive gaze of man.

So after many long and arduous weeks at sea Captain McKinnon brought us safe across the ocean, as he had always promised us he would. We were united in our respect and affection for him, and in our gratitude to him. I shall not forget the morning I first sighted land, the moment I saw the coast of my new country distant on the horizon. I was, as fortune would have it, on watch, high in the crow's-nest, so that it was I who saw her first.

'Land!' I cried. 'On the port bow! America! America!' I recall that moment as amongst the

happiest of my entire life. As I climbed down the rigging to the deck below I heard a fiddle strike up a reel. All day long, as the shore came ever nearer, we danced and sang for sheer joy, and Charlie set up such a howling that we scarce heard the music, a howling to herald not a storm this time, but our triumphant arrival in America.

But our joy was soon to be tempered with sadness, for very shortly after we dropped anchor, Captain McKinnon and I came to the parting of our ways. I heeded his advice to all of us that we should not delay, but leave the ship at once, for, he said, there were Redcoats in America too and they were ever watchful. 'Be always on your guard,' he told us, 'and never forget that it is the cursed Redcoats who hold sway here in America as they do in Scotland. For the most part they keep to the towns, and though they are few in number and the land is vast, yet must you be ever wary. Avoid them, and you will surely find the freedom you seek. May God go with you.'

As we parted that day on the deck of the *Pelican* he thrust his musket into my hand, and told me to go north into the forests, for there the wilderness was the least frequented. 'You will have need of this to survive, Robbie,' he said, 'for it is a wild country you go to and full of many dangers.'

Thus, bidding sad farewells to the Captain and my fellow fugitives, Charlie and I set out on our journey north, making our way by stages into the forests of Vermont where the trees were now ablaze with such a richness of autumn colours as I had never before seen in all my life. Each day we travelled took us ever deeper into this beautiful wilderness. The further we went the fewer people we encountered on the way, and the happier I became. But all the while I kept Charlie clipped and well disguised, for

I was forever anxious that he might be recognized for what he was. Wolves, I reasoned, were likely to be as feared and as loathed here in America as they had been in Scotland, and would therefore be killed on sight.

We lived as we had before in the Highlands, off the land. But here in this new country of plenty, the forests were filled with game of all kinds, with deer and wild pig, with wild turkeys and rabbits, rabbits that were twice, perhaps three times, the size of those I had trapped in Scotland. The rivers and streams also teemed with wondrous strange fish. A man skilled in the arts of hunting and trapping and fishing, as I was, could feed himself forever in such a place. America, as Captain McKinnon had told me was indeed a paradise, a bountiful paradise.

Yet it was a dangerous paradise also, for there were, I soon discovered, bears aplenty in these forests. My first encounter with one such beast proved very nearly to be my last. One evening as Charlie and I sat eating beside my campfire, a great black bear came wandering out of the forest and into the light of our fire, thinking, I supposed, to

share in our feast. My musket was neither near to hand nor loaded. Foolishly, and unlike Charlie who sensibly abandoned me at once and fled, I stood my ground and shouted at the intruder, gesticulating wildly, thinking to frighten him off with my bravado. I did not know then what I know now, that to stand between a hungry bear and his food is most unwise.

Roaring savagely, the bear came running at me,

rearing up to strike me. He would most surely have killed me, and eaten me too, had I not at the very last moment seen the error of my ways and taken to my heels. I later reproached Charlie for his cowardly desertion of me, in reply to which he looked up at me with great disdain in his eyes, reproaching me in return for my stupidity.

Living like a wild man of the woods, hunting and trapping as I went, I was daily seeking out a valley where we might settle and stay, where the land would be good and fertile for farming, where the water was plentiful. But such a place was harder to find than I had imagined. The autumn leaves were falling all about me, and I could already feel the cold of approaching winter in the wind. I knew that time was short, that I had to settle somewhere before winter set in. My search was therefore becoming ever more urgent, ever more desperate.

But I was troubled too by something else. There was, I had begun to perceive, a change in Charlie, in his behaviour, indeed in his whole demeanour. He was now a full grown and adult wolf, and although gentle and kind with me as he had always been, and still a good companion to me, there was, I noted, a look in his eye that had not been there before, a restless faraway look that disturbed me deeply. When we camped at night in the forest, he no longer curled up close beside me, as had always been his custom, but preferred rather to go off on his own and lie down some distance from me. Sometimes he would not sleep at all, but instead would stand and howl at the moon – why, I knew not.

When I awoke in the mornings I would often find him gone. To my great relief he would always return, and when he did, he would greet me most lovingly, as a long-lost friend. For a while at least I was reassured by this show of affection. Yet I knew in my heart that a distance had grown between us, a distance as between father and son, when a son is full-grown and himself becomes a man, when he no longer has any need for a father.

I made camp one evening in a sheltered valley hidden deep in the forest, close to a gently flowing burn where the water was sweet and the fish lay waiting to be caught in the shallows, where I saw both deer and moose come down to drink at dusk.

Here, I resolved, was as good a place to settle and farm as I would ever find. Here we would stay. I had found our home at last, and only just in time.

The first snows of winter were falling as I completed the small log cabin which I hoped would suffice to shelter us from the winter storms. Against the cabin I had piled up wood for the fire, enough I believed to keep the fire burning until the spring. With Captain McKinnon's musket I shot my first bear, a troublesome, scavenging creature who visited the cabin all too often, and quite uninvited. I made good use of his skin to keep me warm on cold winter nights. As for food, I would be able to hunt and trap and fish all we needed.

The winter in Vermont proved bitter cold, with snowstorms that raged about the cabin for days on end, more savage than any I had known in the Highlands. But thankfully the cabin stood firm and was not blown down, though I felt at times it might be. Inside I kept myself warm under my bearskin, and well fed. I had all I needed to survive and should therefore have been quite contented in the sanctuary of my cabin. Yet I was not.

From the very first Charlie would not sleep with me inside the cabin, indeed he rarely ventured inside at all, not even to eat. He would spend his days chasing everything that moved, though catching very little except chipmunks, to which it seemed he had taken a particular liking. Night after night I would lie alone by the fire and listen to his howling outside, hear it echoing through the forest. It was some time before I understood that these were not echoes I was hearing but the answering call of wolves. Only then did it enter my mind that Charlie might one day leave me entirely and go back to his own kind. I tried all I could to banish this possibility from my mind, for the thought of it saddened me deeply. Yet despite my best efforts, this same thought came always back to haunt me, so much so that I lived now in daily dread of losing him.

Although Charlie would go off and leave me, sometimes for days and nights on end, so that I thought never to see him again, yet always he came back to me, and remained my companion throughout all of that first long hard winter. But when he did return, he would not settle. Rather he would stand outside gazing into the forest, his eyes filled with yearning.

I noticed too that he would not now eat what I offered him, and I surmised therefore that he must be hunting for himself. I prayed that he would not leave me entirely but feared now that he would, that the longing in his heart was fast becoming too strong to resist. His loyalty to me, and his instinct to be with his own, were at war inside him, and I knew which of the two must triumph in the end.

One evening in the springtime Charlie came to sit close by me outside the cabin. It was as if he was trying to tell me something, but he could not bring himself to look at me. We were silent together for some time. The chipmunks were at play in the meadow below us, and yet, strangely, he showed no inclination to chase them. I knew then the moment I had dreaded for so long had come at last.

'Go on, Charlie,' said I, with a heavy heart. 'You are free now, as I am. You go wherever you wish. Go where you belong, where you'll be happy. Go.' I pushed him to his feet, then thrust him away from me so that he should be sure of my meaning. Charlie stood and looked back at me for a few moments, and then went away without looking back. I had lost the best friend and companion I ever had in this world and was saddened as never before in my life. Yet I knew that this was how it must be, that fate had brought us here for this parting.

Though I looked for him every day after this, yet I saw Charlie only twice more. The next spring I was clearing the forest, and had made a fire, piling it high with branches and brushwood and roots. I had stopped to rest awhile, to stand back from the great heat, when through the shimmering haze I saw Charlie standing beside the burn. I walked

towards him, calling him to me, but as I approached he stood his ground and watched me warily. A certain look in his eye told me that he did not wish me to come nearer.

I stopped where I was. 'Hello, Charlie,' I said, although so overcome by this time I was barely able to speak. I was pleased to see that he looked fine and strong, and happy in himself, his coat long and wolfish once more. His eyes held mine for a few

fleeting moments before he turned and loped away into the shadows of the forest where at last he disappeared from my view.

I did not think to see him again, but one morning later that same year, as the first of the summer's leaves began to lose their green, Charlie came back to me. This time he was not alone. I can mind I was sitting on the bank of the burn intent upon my fishing when something told me I should look up.

Scarcely a dozen paces from me on the far side of the burn stood two grown wolves and with them four young pups, all as still as statues and gazing back at me.

That the biggest of them was indeed Charlie there could be no doubt, for leaving his family behind him he came padding through the stream to be with me again. As he came up to me I yearned to reach out and stroke him, but held myself back, thinking it not fit to do so, for I knew Charlie was now a wild wolf entirely and would not want the smell of man upon him. He sniffed at the trout lying on the bank beside me, and gave me then a look of such deep affection

that even when I think on it now, all these years later, it brings the tears to my eyes. All too soon he turned away and was gone, taking his family with him, and I was alone. I never set eyes on Charlie again.

Within ten years I had carved my farm out of the forest, and my own sheep grazed in the meadows. I had by now built for myself a handsome house of stone and called the place Burnside. To my great joy I was not to sit alone at my fireside for long, for soon after the house was built I met and married my dear wife Fiona, the only daughter of my nearest neighbour some ten miles away in Woodstock. I brought her home to be with me here at Burnside Farm, where she lived and worked by my side and was my chiefest source of joy and delight for nigh on twenty long and happy years. Together we raised our dear son, Alan – though most tragically we lost two more bairns at birth – before she herself fell ill and died. We buried her in the meadow just below the house, the first field I cleared from the forest after I came to this wondrous valley. That is where I too wish to lie when my turn comes, so that, side by side, we can listen forever to the running of the burn, and the wind in the maple trees, and the howling of the wolves.

* * *

This story I bequeath also to my dear son, Alan, and his descendants, so that they may know and the world will know that the last wolf was not the last wolf.

Resting in Peace

As soon as I was fully recovered from the effects of my pneumonia, I flew off to America, to Boston, to meet my new-found cousin, Marianne.

But I did not go alone.

I asked Miya to come with me because we were in this together, because she and her computer had discovered my roots for me, her roots too. I wanted her with me. It turned out that Marianne and I were both grandparents, and both recent converts to the wonders of computer technology. We found we had much in common.

We decided almost at once – at Miya's suggestion – that we should find Burnside Farm and finish what we had begun. We would see for ourselves the place where Robbie McLeod had chosen to settle. We would stand by the stream where he had last seen Charlie.

It was autumn and the trees were ablaze with glorious colour just as Robbie had described them. After many days of searching, we discovered Burnside Farm, just outside Reading in Vermont. There's a modern farmhouse there now, high on the hill, and across the dirt road from it, a newly built milking parlour that flies the Stars and Stripes from its roof. There are Jersey cows grazing in the fields, a few sheep amongst them, and a herd of beautiful Morgan horses galloping through the meadows. We explained ourselves to the old farmer, who stuffed his hands deep in the pockets of his dungarees and spat a great deal. We asked him where the original farmhouse might have been, and whether we might have a look. He directed us back down the hill towards the stream. He'd never heard of Robbie McLeod, he said, and he didn't seem to be much

interested either, not in Robbie McLeod, nor in the old farmstead. There wasn't much left of it any more, 'just a bunch of old ruins,' he said. But before we left him, he did manage to persuade us to buy a couple of bottles of his best maple syrup. 'Made it myself. Best in Vermont. Best in the whole US of A,' he told us.

'Do you still have wolves around here?' Miya asked him.

'Never seen one,' he replied. 'But I reckon I heard one once, when I was a kid. Too many folks around here these days. They like it wild. You have a good day now, y'hear.' And with that he sent us on our way.

The farmer was right. We found the place without difficulty. Very little of the old farmhouse remained at all, just a few stone walls, no more than head high anywhere, a fireplace, and a crumbling chimney stack. Mature maple trees grew now within the ruined walls of the old house. There wasn't much more to see, so we walked down towards the stream, and stood on the spot where we thought Robbie McLeod might last have seen Charlie. We stayed as long as we could, not wanting to leave at all. It was coming on to dusk, when quite by chance, Miya came across the grave, a great slab of slate, now cracked and crooked. Crouching down, she brushed away the leaves. The words were still just legible in the last glow of day.

Here lie Robbie McLeod and Fiona McLeod
beloved father and mother
of Alan
Resting in Peace

We stood over them for a few moments, then left them to their peace and went away.

AUTHOR'S NOTE

Ever since I first read *Kidnapped* by Robert Louis Stevenson, I have been fascinated and horrified by the story of Bonnie Prince Charlie and his Jacobite rebellion of 1745. I think that's why I have always wanted to write a story set in these turbulent times.

The opportunity came when a friend of mine told me of an extraordinary discovery he had made way up in the north of Scotland. It seems he came across a stone on which was written: 'Near this spot was killed the last wolf in Scotland'. I later found out that there at least six other places in Scotland that claim the same thing. What we know for certain is that the last wild wolf did indeed disappear from Scotland either in the 17th or 18th centuries. Wolves were hunted down and wiped out, in much the same way, I thought, as the rebels who fought for Bonnie Prince Charlie against the Redcoats. I called my idea for the story *The Last Wolf* – it's not often I find a title before I write the story – did some historical research about the rebellion and its aftermath, and then began to weave my tale.

Some historical background: in 1688, the last of the Stuart kings, James II, was forced off the throne of England. His grandson, Bonnie Prince Charlie, returned to reclaim the throne in 1745. He landed on the remote coast of North-West Scotland where he was greeted enthusiastically by his followers. These supporters of his cause were called 'Jacobites' – Jacobus being the Latin for James.

Bonnie Prince Charlie moved down through Scotland gathering an army as he went. He reached Edinburgh where he was fêted for a month as King, and then he moved south into England. But before long his army began to wither away. He got almost as far as Derby, but his army was now in serious disarray and he had to retreat north again to Scotland. Here at Culloden Moor his army of Highlanders and other Jacobite supporters was routed by the Redcoat Hanoverian forces of King George II of England, led by the Duke of Cumberland, or 'Butcher' Cumberland. He was known as 'Butcher' Cumberland because he sent out his Redcoats to hunt down all the rebels, their sympathizers and their families. Massacring and burning as they went, their cruelty was terrible.

As a result, many Scottish people fled their country, and some took refuge in Canada and in America. At this time both Canada and America were still British colonies, and therefore garrisoned by British Redcoats who defended the territory from the French.

As for Bonnie Prince Charlie, he escaped from Culloden Moor, helped on his way to France by Flora MacDonald – but that's another story, or another legend.

ABOUT THE AUTHOR

Michael Morpurgo was born in St Albans in 1943. As a child he wrote occasionally for his prep-school magazine, but he had no intention of becoming a writer. At the age of thirteen, Michael went to King's School, Canterbury having won a scholarship for being, as he says, 'a good all-round sort of chap'.

After a brief spell at Sandhurst Military Academy, Michael gained a degree of what he calls 'distinctly inferior quality' at Kings College, London and went into teaching. It was as a teacher that Michael began making up stories to tell his class. By great good fortune, Michael had one of the stories accepted by a publisher. Michael considers *War Horse,* published in 1982, to have been his breakthrough book.

Michael now has over 90 titles to his name and is recognized as 'one of today's greatest storytellers' *(Bookseller)*. He has written for every age group and joined forces with several well-known illustrators. His books have won a clutch of awards including the Whitbread Award, the IBBY Honour Book, the Writer's Guild Award, the Children's Book Award and the Smarties Prize.

With Ted Hughes, he was instrumental in setting up the Children's Laureate in order to encourage a wider appreciation and love of the best in children's literature.

Michael's other books for Doubleday/Corgi are *The Rainbow Bear,* also illustrated by Michael Foreman, and *The Silver Swan,* with illustrations by Christian Birmingham, *Tom's Sausage Lion* and *Black Queen*.

As well as writing, Michael also founded the charity Farms for City Children with his wife, Clare, for which they were both awarded the MBE in 1999. In 2001 Michael was made a fellow of Kings College, an institution which obviously doesn't hold his first degree against him! Michael and Clare live in Devon and have three children and six grandchildren.

ABOUT THE ILLUSTRATOR

Michael Foreman was born in Suffolk in 1938. Now recognized as one of the most outstanding contemporary British illustrators, he started attending art college two afternoons a week while still at school. He went on to study full-time at Lowestoft Art School, then at St Martin's College in London and the Royal College of Art, where he received a first-class degree in Graphics. After his studies, he worked in the USA and in Britain as a magazine art director but always continued working on ideas for children's books. His very first book for children, *The General*, was published in 1961. Since then Michael has illustrated scores of books by authors as diverse as Shakespeare, Terry Jones and Kenneth Grahame.

He is one of the handful of illustrators to have been awarded the Kate Greenaway Medal twice (in 1983 and 1990). He has also won the Smarties Prize, the Children's Book Award and the Kurt Maschler Award. His illustrations have enhanced many classic stories such as *Peter Pan* and *The Jungle Book* and re-tellings of legends too, including *The Saga of Erik the Viking*. Michael has also written the texts for many of his best known books, such as the early *Dinosaurs and all that Rubbish*, a story about conservation, and the highly acclaimed trilogy based on his own family's wartime experiences, *War Boy*, *After the War Was Over* and *War Game*.

Michael's vivid illustrations have long been associated with Michael Morpurgo's fascinating and moving stories and *The Last Wolf* is their second book together for Doubleday.

Michael Foreman now lives part of the year in London and part on the coast, in Cornwall, inspiration for many of his famous seascape illustrations. He is married and has two sons.